Benjamin's Barn

For Benjamin, of course! R.L.

For Atha Tehon, Art Director—
my work is always enhanced by her light touch. S.J.

PUFFIN PIED PIPER BOOKS
Published by the Penguin Group
Penguin Books USA Inc., 375 Hudson Street, New York, New York 10014, U.S.A.
Penguin Books Ltd, 27 Wrights Lane, London W8 5TZ, England
Penguin Books Australia Ltd, Ringwood, Victoria, Australia
Penguin Books Canada Ltd, 10 Alcorn Avenue, Toronto, Ontario, Canada M4V 3B2
Penguin Books (N.Z.) Ltd, 182-190 Wairau Road, Auckland 10, New Zealand
Penguin Books Ltd, Registered Offices: Harmondsworth, Middlesex, England

Originally published in hardcover by
Dial Books for Young Readers
A Division of Penguin Books USA Inc.

BENJAMIN'S BARN
is also published in hardcover editions by
Dial Books for Young Readers.

Benjamin's Barn

REEVE LINDBERGH
paintings *by* SUSAN JEFFERS

A Puffin Pied Piper

Benjamin's barn
Is so big and so warm
He could shelter an elephant
Safe from a storm

Or nestle a lamb
That's just barely been born
(Because Benjamin's barn
Is enormously warm).

Benjamin's barn
Is so big and so tall
He could hide a whole pirate ship there—
Mast and all!

Or an old piebald horse
In a high-ceilinged stall
(Because Benjamin's barn
Is enormously tall).

Benjamin's barn
Is so big and so wide
He could easily keep
Pterodactyls inside

Or a dozen plump pigeons
Arranged side by side
(Because Benjamin's barn
Is enormously wide).

Benjamin's barn
Is so big and so soft
He could ask a frail princess
To sleep in the trough

Or a pair of raccoons
To curl up in the loft
(Because Benjamin's barn
Is enormously soft).

Benjamin's barn
Is so big and so grand
He could call up the mayor
To send a brass band

Or just have ten geese
And a gander on hand
(Because Benjamin's barn
Is enormously grand).

Benjamin's barn
Is so big and so clean
He could hold a great ball
For the king and the queen

Or the cow and the bull
And the milking machine
(Because Benjamin's barn
Is enormously clean).

Benjamin's barn
Is so big and so neat
He could toss a rhinoceros in
For a treat

Or a bossy old billygoat
Quick on his feet
(Because Benjamin's barn
Is enormously neat).

But...Benjamin's barn
Is so big and so full
With the horse, cow, goat, pigeons,
Raccoons, sheep, geese, bull,

That he thinks he won't ask the rest in
After all
(Because Benjamin's barn
Is enormously full)!

REEVE LINDBERGH

is the author of *Midnight Farm*, also illustrated by Susan Jeffers, which was a *Publishers Weekly* Children's Bestseller, a *Booklist* Children's Editors' Choice, and a *Redbook* Best Children's Picture Books of the Year award winner. She is also the author of *The Day the Goose Got Loose*, illustrated by Steven Kellogg, which received a *Booklist* starred review. Her most recent book, *There's a Cow in the Road*, was illustrated by Tracey Campbell Pearson. Ms. Lindbergh lives in St. Johnsbury, Vermont.

SUSAN JEFFERS

is the acclaimed illustrator of *Brother Eagle, Sister Sky: A Message from Chief Seattle* (Dial), a *New York Times* Bestseller, winner of the 1992 ABBY Award (the American Booksellers Association's Book of the Year), and *Parents* Magazine's Best Children's Book of 1991. Ms. Jeffers's other books for Dial include Reeve Lindbergh's *Midnight Farm*, a *Booklist* Children's Editors' Choice; Longfellow's *Hiawatha*, a *School Library Journal* Best Book of the Year; and four fairy tales retold by Amy Ehrlich: *Cinderella, The Snow Queen, Thumbelina,* and *The Wild Swans*, each an *American Bookseller* Pick of the Lists, among other honors. Her most recent book for Dial is *Waiting for the Evening Star*, written by Rosemary Wells, about which *Booklist* noted, "Wells and Jeffers vividly capture a sense of a time gone by in this warm-hearted story...."